AAM 6255
·12.95
m48

D1315395

DISCARDED BY
MEMPHIS PUBLIC LIBRARY

AAM 6255
·12.95
m48

Noel the Coward

by Robert Kraus

illustrated by Jose Aruego and Ariane Dewey

Simon and Schuster Books for Young Readers
Published by Simon & Schuster Inc., New York

Simon and Schuster Books for Young Readers
Simon & Schuster Building
1230 Avenue of the Americas
New York, New York, 10020

Text copyright © 1977 by Robert Kraus
Illustrations copyright © 1977 by Jose Aruego and Ariane Dewey
All rights reserved including the right of reproduction
in whole or in part in any form.
Published by the Simon & Schuster Juvenile Division
SIMON AND SCHUSTER BOOKS FOR YOUNG READERS
is a trademark of Simon & Schuster Inc.
Manufactured in the United States of America

10 9 8 7 6 5 4 3 2   10 9 8 7 6 5 4 3 2   (Pbk)

Library of Congress Cataloging-in-Publication Data

Kraus, Robert 1925–
Noel, the coward / by Robert Kraus;
illustrated by Jose Aruego and Ariane Dewey.
p. cm.
Summary: Coward powered Noel changes to a hero with the help of
Charlie's School of Self Defense.
[1. Courage—Fiction.] I. Aruego, Jose, ill. II. Dewey, Ariane,
ill. III. Title.
PZ7.K868No 1988
[E]—dc19
88-3192   CIP   AC
ISBN: 0-671-66845-5   0-671-66846-3 (Pbk)

For Charles C. Nelson
Former Instructor
U.S. Marines

Noel was a coward.

So was his father.

"Better a live coward than a dead hero," said Noel's mother.

But Noel wasn't happy being a live coward.

Gus and Tony
punched and teased him.
"Noel, Noel,
Is a coward!

Noel, Noel's
Coward powered,"
they shouted,
throwing sticks and stones.

Noel ran away crying.
"I'm not a coward!
I just don't know
how to fight back!"

"Neither do I,"
said Noel's father.

So they both went to
Charlie's School of Self-Defense.

Charlie was little but tough.
"The bigger they are, the harder I fall,"
he said, shadowboxing. "I mean, the harder
they fall!" he corrected himself.
"Notice my fancy footwork!"

"Can you teach us?" asked Noel.
"You bet," said Charlie.

Noel and his father learned

boxing,

wrestling,   judo,

karate,

kung fu,

and dirty fighting!
"It often comes in handy," said Charlie.

They graduated with honors!

The next day Gus and Tony
punched and teased Noel.

Noel dodged their punches
and ignored their teasing.

He snapped his fingers, gave them
a dirty look and walked away.

He didn't have to fight them
because he *knew* he could!

Gus and Tony knew he could, too,
and they never punched and teased Noel again.
Or Noel's father.

"My heroes!" said Noel's mother.

And they really were.